LIGHTS OUT
Book 2

By Nathan Reese Maher

1st Edition, February 2017
2nd Edition, November 2017
Copyright © 2017, Nathan Reese Maher

Cover Artist & Illustrations:
Tobie-Marie White
Editor: Harley Maher
Proofreader: Judy Kingyon

LIGHTS OUT, BOOK 2, All Rights Reserved

Printed in the United States.

ISBN – 978-1-965179-24-6

This book is published in Open Dyslexic Font provided commercially free from https:/ /opendyslexic.org

Chapter 1

"On your marks!" Abby shouted from the side walk.

All the kids had cleared off from the street and observed from a safe distance. No one knew what to expect.

Lydia edged closer to the starting line. The child who could control her long blonde hair like hands had drawn a crude line across the pavement with chalk.

Shelly quickly checked the bottom of her shoes for any rocks that could slow her down. Just like her coach had instructed her, she kneeled down so she could push off the pavement as soon as the signal was given.

"Get set..." Abby called out.

Thomas was nervous. He kept close to Abby, clutching Percy, his rabbit, tightly to his chest. Percy worried about how the outcome of the race would affect his child.

Shelly steadied her breathing so that the moment Abby gave the word she would explode into a sprint.

Lydia revved her engine just to intimidate Shelly. "Be prepared to lose, Whinny." She taunted from her grill.

Shelly was irritated, especially now since Lydia had swallowed a car and transformed into one. Now, Lydia was far louder and obnoxious than before.

"GO!"

Shelly launched herself into a sprint as Lydia tore down the street, zooming by Shelly immediately.

Lydia laughed at how quickly she got ahead and shouted back, "So long – LOSER!"

Not about to give up this early, Shelly kept running. Just as she had several times before, the more her shoes hit the pavement the brighter her feet became. As they glowed, she felt the world as it pushed beneath her; it was a feeling as if the heated air created a pocket for her to run on. She knew her speed would only increase.

As soon as Lydia made her first turn at the end of the street, Shelly was already catching up.

"Get her, Shell!" Abby shouted ecstatically.
Thomas could not help but be caught in the excitement. "Go! Go!" He yelled, but he wasn't sure who he was rooting for. Maybe he would get lucky and the race would end in a tie and he could remain friends with everyone. He was shocked when Lydia had used him as part of a bet – one that stated

whoever won would get Thomas and the other person had to stop being his friend. He didn't think it was fair at all, and it bothered him a lot.

As Shelly reached the turn, she pivoted on her heel without missing a beat. Meanwhile, Lydia had to slow down in order to make the turn safely. Even so, her tires skidded loudly against the pavement.

While Lydia kept one eye focused on the road, she tried to keep her other eye on her rearview mirror.   She hadn't realized that Shelly could keep building speed and it seemed like there was a limit. On foot, Lydia knew she could beat Shelly, but Shelly's patch gave her a tremendous advantage.

It just isn't fair! Lydia thought. Shelly was gaining on her and it wouldn't be long before she'd reach the other turn. *She HAS to be cheating!*

The sole remaining Gaines knew she had to do whatever it took to win.

Turning the corner, Lydia lost a few additional seconds to Shelly, just as before. As soon as Lydia was in the clear, she boosted her speed, causing her engine to roar. The sound echoed loudly across the neighborhood.

To Shelly, the houses passed by in a blur and the lines on the street became one solid streak of white. Shelly made the turn perfectly, but as she was about to hit the new street, she stumbled slightly; enough where it caused the pavement to crack. Her foot skidded and ripped up concrete, which built up in a pile around her heel. Shelly used it to kick off from to ensure she was able to stay in the race. Her feet now glowed so brightly that they burst into bluish flames which flickered wildly behind her.

Shelly came up to Lydia's bumper in seconds but when she attempted to pass, Lydia veered into her to cut her off.

"Woah! Watch it—!" Shelly cried out.

Her heart leapt into her throat, her feet landed wrong and immediately Shelly's shoes skipping her down the street like a rock across a pond. Shelly didn't know how to stop herself; she was certain she'd fall and worse – with her shoes the way they were – she knew she was going to crash into something or someone! Desperate, she tried to correct herself, but instead her feet kicked up from under her and the pavement came up fast. Shelly closed her eyes and braced for impact!

Chapter 2

When there wasn't a crash, Shelly cautiously opened her eyes. Her body was still, she was no longer running or even on the street for that matter. She was surrounded by branches and leaves.

Somehow, she had landed in a tree!

Lydia saw that Shelly had lost her footing, possibly even crashed, as she could no longer see her. *Good riddance,* Lydia thought as she breathed a sigh of relief. She grinned as best as a car could. *I've finally knock that smirk off Shelly's face. Now everyone will know I'm the fastest.*

Upon nearing the third turn, something big and yellow appeared directly in front of Lydia. It was a person and they were going to collide! Lydia turned sharply to the right. She skidded across the road and spun out into someone's front yard. In all the chaos, Lydia lost control of her stomach and she threw up the car that she swallowed earlier. The vehicle landed unharmed near her as she planted face first onto the grass.

Confused on how she got there to begin with, Shelly adjusted herself and climbed down the tree. Thomas spotted her first, as he was only a few houses away.

"Hey! What were you doing in a tree? You're supposed to be racing." He laughed loud enough that it captured everyone's attention.

Shelly took another glance at the tree, trying to figure out the answer herself, before she began her brief trek towards the awaiting children. Suddenly someone grabbed her shoulder and she was jerked instantly to them.

She cried out in surprise and, for a moment, she felt as if she was going to fall over.

"Whoa! Who is *she*?" Abby asked.

The person was just lifting their hand off Shelly when she was able to identify who it was, it was that yellow dress girl from the other day.

"Aloha Oukou. It looked like your soul was escaping so I put you in a tree. My name is Haukea, in case you forgot."

Nervous, Shelly replied, "I-I remember you, Haukea. YOU put me in that tree?" She asked in disbelief.

"Yes – and here you are whole again, ku'u momi makamae."

"How did you do that?" Abby asked excitedly.

One of the gawking children, the six-year old with the long hair, echoed Abby. "Yes! How did you do that?"

"I just step and the world moves beneath my feet, which is very kind of it. I sometimes fear I'd fall off of it if it didn't."

"So..." Shelly was a bit confused. "Do you teleport, like Felicity Bell of the Wonderkins?" The Wonderkins was one of the few TV shows she watched religiously.

"No. I step. The Earth moves. That's it."

"That's like me!" Said the smaller Mendoza boy. "I open a door and I can go to any other door that I know."

Haukea blinked a few times. "That sounds different. I can see it as very important though."

A voice erupted over their conversation. "You nearly killed me!" Lydia accused as she stomped in their direction. Her clothes were covered in grass stains. Her face was red and her eyes narrowed at Haukea.

"What happened, Leedee?" Percy asked as he leapt to the ground from Thomas' arms.

Lydia Gaines pointed her finger with rage at Haukea. "You stood in the middle of the street on purpose! You made me crash!"

The older Mendoza sister spoke up. "Sounds like you almost killed *her*. Do you even have a driver's license?"

"What?! Don't be ridiculous! I'm not old enough to have a driver's license. Why would I have one?"

The smaller girl in the purple dress and the bubble parasol snottily remarked, "Well you shouldn't be driving if you don't have a license."

"I wasn't driving a car. I *was* the car! I don't need a license to drive myself!"

"You were still *driving*." The boy taunted; his dark hair hidden beneath his baseball hat.

"Ugh!" The rich blonde roared. "You're all so frustrating! I hate you." She pointed at Shelly. "Don't think this is over! I'm the fastest and everyone knows it!" She stalked away. "Come on, Thomas! We're leaving!"

Thomas picked Percy back up and squeezed him tightly. He didn't budge.

His cousin briefly halted her tantrum. "Thomas! We're going!" She repeated harshly.

He finally shook his head. "I want to stay here." He said in a small whisper.

"What did you say!?" Lydia shouted more out of disbelief than because she hadn't heard him.

Thomas shrank into himself and started to cry.

Percy spoke for him. "Sir Thomas doesn't wish to go with you, Lydia."

Her eyes narrowed as if her little cousin had betrayed her. "Fine! I'm better off without you anyways." She turned away and kept walking without looking back.

Shelly went down on her knee to look Thomas in the eyes. "Are you okay?"

Abby quickly joined them too, wanting to show him that she was there for him if he needed her.

Thomas sniffed to hold back his tears. "Something's wrong." He inhaled. "Leedee is never this mean."

"Lydia has been nothing but mean to us, Shell, but I think Thomas is right. She was way meaner than usual. She even bet Thomas in a race. Who would do that?" Abby asked as she fidgeted with one of her braids.

"You may both be right." Shelly contemplated. "I should go back and have a talk with Arthur and Mindy. They may know more about that patch Mindy had sewn onto Lydia's soul."

"Patch?" The girl in the purple dress asked.

"Oh – Um…" Shelly paused in realization that most everyone didn't know. "The reason we have these powers is because there are patches stitched on to our souls. We found one and Lydia had it sewn on by a girl who works at the SOK Market."

"So… You think there's something bad with these patches?" The girl let go of her parasol that she had copied from the Mendoza sister. The parasol changed back into a string of bubbles and they all popped at once.

"I'm not sure." Shelly shrugged. "What I do know is that anyone who has their eighteenth birthday turns into a monster. That's what happened to Lydia brother. He tried to eat us."

The long-haired first-grader began to shake. She hugged her teddy bear tightly. "Monsters?! How did you get away?"

Shelly looked back at Thomas and decided it wasn't the best time to talk about it. "I'll tell you all later, okay?" She stood back up once she noticed that Thomas was in better spirits.

"Okay!" The little girl smiled widely. "My name is Clarissa Betterman. What's yours?"

"Shelly Wynn." She replied.

"I'm Ximena Mendoza and this is my brother Javier Maximiliano Mendoza." Offered the girl in the fluffy black dress with the white trim.

"Don't call me Javier." He petitioned his sister. "Call me Max, okay?"

The girl with the ebony skin smoothed out her purple dress. "I'm Jasmine King."

"I'm Fang Gan." Said the boy in the baseball cap who had whistled for them earlier.

"I'm Abby McMullen. This is Thomas LeRue and Sir Percy Rabbit." She laughed.

Clarissa wrapped her hair around her like a blanket. "Shelly?"

"Yeah?" Shelly replied after Thomas wiped his eyes on his sleeve and gave a small smile.

"I'm hungry."

Shelly looked to Thomas and then to everyone else before settling on Abby. "Can you help Clarissa? I should take Thomas back to the SOK Market to get some answers about his cousin."

"No sweat!" Abby stated. "Everyone can come to my place for some peanut butter and jelly sandwiches." Abby took Clarissa by the hand. "And Shell... please be careful. That place gives me the creeps."

Shelly gave Abby a thumbs up. "I'll do my best." Shelly remembered that she should thank Haukea for saving her but when she looked back to where she had previously been standing, Shelly realized she had vanished.

"Well Thomas," Shelly asked as she took one last look around for the girl in the yellow dress. "Are you and Percy ready to go?"

Percy nodded and Thomas managed a thumbs up.

Chapter 3

"Are you doing any better?" Shelly asked she and Thomas pushed their bicycles along the side of the street.

"I guess so." His voice was glum, and he kept his eyes to the sidewalk.

Percy rode in Thomas' front bicycle basket. He faced both of them; one ear drooped but the other was perked.

Thomas took a few moments before he looked up at Shelly. "Do you think there's something wrong with Leedee's patch?"

"I don't know." Shelly replied, unsure of what to say. She adjusted her hula hoop on her shoulder. "I mean... she's not the friendliest person at school."

Percy joined in. "Leedee has always been the best to us. She's kind, considerate and has never let us down. Well..." His ears twitched. "At least not until today. Circumstances being as they are."

Thomas nodded his head. "You're right, Percy. She's always been nice to us."

"Oh—" Shelly stopped for a moment and realized that perhaps it wasn't best to sour his perception of his cousin. "Well... that's probably because you're such a great cousin. I can't imagine anyone being mean to you, even Lydia for that matter."

Thomas smiled widely. "You really think so?"

"Of course – you are great!" The rabbit exclaimed as he leaned against the wall of the basket. "You are a wondrous child with many fantastic traits. You should be proud of who you are."

Thomas couldn't contain his happiness and he giggled. "Thanks, you two!" He took a moment to allow his laughter to wear itself out before speaking again. "For a little while, I thought there was something wrong with me."

"No!" Shelly blurted out. It frustrated her that Lydia had made him think that about himself. "There's nothing wrong with you at all. Sometimes people say or do things that are mean because there's something the matter with them. With Lydia, it seems there's always something wrong with her."

"Like what?" Thomas asked with concern.

Shelly worried that she may have said too much. "I-I'm not sure exactly."

The truth was, Shelly had never thought about it. Lydia had always come across as someone who was constantly aimed at distressing others. In fact, hearing that she's been nice to others was really surprising to her.

"Maybe I should find out." She thought out loud.

"That's a very brave thing to do, Lady Shelly." Percy commended.

"Brave? How so?"

"You're seeking to understand the root of her misgivings. Perhaps recognizing the cause, you two can find a way to mend the rift between you. That's being brave."

"I'll be honest, Percy. I've never really considered it until just now."

"You obviously care about her." Thomas jumped in. "Why else would you go through all this trouble to help her?"

Care about Lydia Gaines? Shelly asked herself. "Maybe I do." She admitted openly.

The idea of sitting around when someone was in pain, especially if there was something she could do about it, just didn't sit well with her.

They came across the location where the SOK Market had been earlier that morning. The neon sign still shone brightly, despite it being early in the afternoon. The house looked as dilapidated as ever, and felt far more sinister than it had the first time they encountered it.

"Do you think they'll let us in?" Thomas asked as he looked the house over.

"I don't see why not." Shelly affirmed. "They let us in last time."

"Last time we had an invitation." Percy reminded them.

Shelly put up the kickstand to her bike and unslung her hoop she had been carrying with her the entire way.
"I'm sure it'll be okay. I don't see much of a line, do you?" Shelly jokingly pointed out.

"Nope!" Thomas concluded with joy.

Cautiously, Shelly approached the front door. Just as Lydia had, she let herself in. The door knocked into a bell to announce their arrival.   Shelly was careful to hold the door open so that Thomas and Percy could easily follow her inside.

The lobby was empty. The front desk was vacant.

"Hello?" Shelly called out awkwardly. After no answer she asked, "I wonder where he is."

"Maybe he's in the bathroom." Thomas exclaimed.

Shelly chuckled. "Why do you say that?"

"I kind of need to go." He giggled.

Percy looked around. "I don't know where they would keep one. It may be impolite to use it without asking."

Shelly examined some of the adjoining doors in the foyer. She attempted the knobs but found that the doors were locked.

"No luck there." She tried a few others and encountered the same problem. "That's strange. Why was the front door unlocked and the sign still on if no one is here?"

Percy's ears twitched and he looked up to where the stairs led up to the higher floors. "Maybe that Arthur fellow is upstairs."

Thomas and Shelly both glanced up to where the rabbit had suggested. The velvet rope that previously blocked it off was unhooked and dangled to the floor. A red carpet ran up the stairs like a giant tongue.

"Well, the rope is down, so it must be okay, right?" Thomas asked.

Shelly shrugged her shoulders with a reassuring smile. "I don't see a sign that says otherwise, so it must be. Let's try upstairs. Maybe we can find Arthur that way."

"And a bathroom!" Thomas asserted happily.

"That too!" Shelly agreed. She wandered to the base of the stairs. She adjusted the hula hoop on her shoulder and stared up at the shadows of the upper floor.

The walls were plastered with a faded floral wallpaper with square spots on the wall where picture frames once hung. There were gas-fed wall sconces that reached out to grab anyone who strayed too close to the wall. Shelly only knew about them because she went on the 7th grade field trip to Laliz

Pouce's mansion on the bluffs on the east side of town. Her mansion had similar looking wall fixtures.

Sighing, Shelly slowly started up the stairs.

"Shelly?" Thomas asked from behind her while she pondered the possibility of ghosts.

"Huh?"

"Do you carry your hoop with you everywhere?"

Shelly placed a hand on the back of her head and blushed. "I didn't used to. Since everything that happened with Alex I feel a lot safer with it."

"I think that's a very good reason to carry it." Percy offered as he walked up the first step.

She appreciated the reassurance. "Thanks Percy, it's nice to know I'm not being irrational."

With a quick breath and a hesitant look back to the vacant desk, Shelly continued up the stairs. Each step creaked, and a couple boards rattled as if the nails were coming loose. Thomas and Percy followed close behind, keeping their hands on the railing for support.

At the top was a long hallway fit with several doors and another set of stairs at the end that went even higher into the house. The walls were stained and barren. The carpet on the floor was worn in small places revealing the floorboards underneath. The first door to their left, nearest the stairs, was open wide enough for them to recognize the bathroom.

"Well, there's no Arthur, but there's a bathroom." Shelly announced.

Thomas peered into the room and then nodded his head cheerfully.

"Are you going to need any help?" Shelly asked.

"Nope! I can manage a-okay!" He giggled and gave her the thumbs up before going inside and shutting the door behind him.

Percy placed his hand on his sword and scanned the room with his eyes; ears alert for any noise.

"Are you okay? You look a little nervous." She asked.

"I'm standing guard. One can't be too careful." Percy kept his gaze on the hallway. "This place has an unusual smell about it, and there is so much settling in the home... it's hard to tell what is happening."

She took a moment to breathe through her nose to see what he meant. All that Shelly could smell was dust.

"You mean that old house smell?"

"No..." The rabbit paused. "There's something here that I haven't smelled before. Something different and foul."

Shelly shifted her foot with uneasiness and her shoe scrapped against plaster. She looked down at the small pile at her feet and then up at the ceiling. There were hanging lights suspended by chains. Large cracks in the ceiling had gathered around their bases. It was as if something had tried pulling the lights out of the sockets.

Shelly began imagining all sorts of terrors that could have the strength to pull them out – let alone be able to reach that high.

A smashing sound came from further down the hallway. Their eyes rested on a pair of sliding doors.

"That sounded like a dish." Percy whispered.

"Yeah..." Shelly retorted. "Stay here okay?"

Percy nodded.

Shelly took her hoop off her shoulder and tucked it behind her arm to allow her a quick spin if she needed to. She did her best to be as silent as possible. Despite her efforts, a step landed on a weak point in the floor and the boards moaned. Shelly stopped and listened; when nothing stirred, she continued nervously on her way.

When she reached the sliding doors, she slowly extended her hand out to see if she could push one aside. The toilet flushed and she twisted back to see if everything was okay. The sliding doors opened, and Shelly whirled back around to find herself face to face with a figure. They yelped in surprise, causing Shelly to shriek and stumble backwards. Shelly tripped over the carpet and fell to the ground with an "Ow!".

Chapter 4

"Oh my gosh, I am so sorry!" It was Mindy. She hastily closed the door behind her and offered Shelly a hand up.

"It's okay. I'm okay." Shelly reassured while rubbing her behind. Once the pain eased, Shelly grabbed Mindy's hand and together they pulled her to her feet.

The door to the bathroom opened and Thomas walked out. "All better!" He announced.

Mindy looked between the three of them and asked, "What are you doing here?"

"We have some questions about patches but then we heard a noise. Is everything okay?

The thirteen-year-old glanced behind her. "I'm just clumsy is all. It's fine. You can't be up here though, it's against the rules."

"Really? How come?" Shelly inquired.

"Because," she said as they walked back towards the stairs where Thomas and Percy waited. "The owner doesn't want any children up here without his permission."

"The owner? Like an adult?"

Mindy didn't answer her; instead, she started down the stairs. "Come on. You said you had questions? I'm a patch expert. We can talk downstairs."

Shelly raised an eyebrow, turned to Thomas and silently begged him for his thoughts on the matter.

"Sounds good to me." Thomas accepted with a shrug.

She stole one last suspicious glance back at the sliding doors before Shelly gave in and

followed the raven-haired girl back downstairs.

Once they returned to the lobby, Mindy released a sigh of relief. "Now, what questions do you have?"

Shelly stole a look back upstairs. She wasn't buying Mindy's explanation of the noise she heard. Mindy was also very insistent that they couldn't be upstairs. *If there aren't any adults around, what would it matter?*

"So, who is the owner of the SOK Market?" Shelly asked with caution.

"I'm not allowed to talk about it. It's..." She looked to the side for the right words. "A very private person. I'm sure you'll meet it when it's ready." Mindy was quick to change the subject. "You said something about patches?"

"Right – do you remember the girl from earlier this morning? You sewed on a patch for her."

"The loud, rude one? Blonde hair?"

"Yes – her!" Shelly was glad she wasn't alone by thinking that Lydia had no manners. "I'm worried that the patch is making her more – difficult – than she normally is. Is that possible?"

Mindy crossed her arms. "Well... we all have patches, but I haven't really sewn too many of them to say exactly. I was told that patches carry their own burdens and having too many of them – especially when you're not ready – can cause some problems."

"I knew it!" Shelly exclaimed with pride. Her cheeks flushed with embarrassment for being so boisterous. "Sorry... what kind of problems?"

Thomas walked over to an old circle-back chair resting against the wall beneath a painting of a city in the middle of the ocean. He climbed up on the chair to sit. His feet didn't quite reach the ground and, once situated, he kicked them back and forth while listening.

"Patches don't look it, but when attached to your soul they can get pretty heavy. They go over the holes in your soul, like when you patch a sock. When you have a hole in your soul, it's because you're hurting from something. I don't know if you noticed, but that girl had a lot of holes."

"I'm not sure I understand. Are you saying that Lydia is in a lot of pain?" Shelly was struck by how absurd that sounded. From her perspective, Lydia was too busy causing pain to others to be suffering from any herself.

"Hey?" Thomas asked. "May I have one of these?"

Thomas had found a dish filled with small individually wrapped pieces of taffy on a nearby side table.

Mindy beamed a smile to him. "Of course! I just put those out. I'd rather you enjoy them than Arthur."

"Anyways," Mindy pulled them back into the conversation. "You know when you go to the doctor and you get a shot, and if you look away it doesn't hurt as much? Then you get a bandage, and every time you see it you're reminded that you got a shot and how much it hurt to begin with? It's kind of like that."

"I think I get it. Patches can remind us of pain. Like the first time I fell off my bike or

SOK
MARKET

something?"

Mindy sighed with a reassuring smile. "Well, something more painful... like being left behind by your parents, never having any e-mails or text messages answered when you're lonely, or being placed in a boarding school because no one wants you around."

"That's awful!" Shelly exclaimed. "Who would do that?"

Mindy bit her lip. "Don't worry – they, ah, they were just examples."

Shelly gave a sigh of relief.

"Anywho, when all you have is pain, you turn into a shadow of who you once were. When a patch is put over a hole, it just covers it up, makes you stop feeling it as much, but it's still there."

"So why would anyone want another patch? Arthur seemed so eager to have Lydia stitch hers on." Shelly asked with concern as she recalled how insistent Arthur had been.

Mindy shrugged. "They are neat to have. You just have to be strong." She placed her hand over her heart. "Pain can also help you face who you are, but not everyone can do it on their own. Some people need a lot of support and patience."

"Is... Is Lydia in trouble?"

"If she's having problems with her patches, she's in more trouble than she's ever been in. Our shadow selves... I can't imagine being in more frightening company."

"We need to go find her." Shelly exclaimed loud enough so that Thomas and Percy could hear her.

"Just be careful." Mindy warned. "She may not want your help. That's the worst of it, especially since she needs it."

"Lydia is a real pain, but Thomas is her cousin, so I need to make sure that she's okay."

Mindy nodded. "Okay. If you need anything let me know. I'll be here." Mindy started her way back up the stairs and Shelly followed her with her eyes.

Once at the first few steps, the black dressed seamstress stopped and leaned over the railing. "If Lydia needs it, I can take the patch off. She's the one who has to make that decision though. I can't take off a patch unless the other person wants me to."

It was now Shelly's turn to nod. "I'll be sure to let her know." She pivoted on her foot to check on Thomas who now sat side by side with Percy, swinging their feet back and forth while Thomas was enjoying taffy.

"Come on Thomas, let's go look for Lydia okay?"

The young boy smiled from the delicious snack. "Okay!" He mumbled as he shifted the taffy to the other side of his mouth so he could speak.

Percy jumped off the chair and adjusted the wooden sword at his belt. "Thank you very much for your help, Lady Mindy." Percy stated once Thomas joined up with Shelly as she moved off towards the front door. They exited together.

Shelly stepped off the porch and glanced at the second story window. The dirt was thick on the glass making it hard for her to see inside. She heard a faint crash, as if someone had broken something larger this time.

"Where do we go now?" Thomas asked.

"We need to find where Lydia went. Do you think that she returned home?" Shelly asked more as a means to confirm her own suspicions.

"Maybe." Thomas replied. "That's where I always find her."

Still in doubt, Shelly said, "It couldn't hurt to look I guess."

They both walked over to their bicycles and climbed on the seat. "Come on! Let's see if we can find her."

Chapter 5

They went to Lydia's house and knocked repeatedly on the door, but Lydia never answered. The house was dark inside, and Shelly couldn't see Lydia's bike anywhere.

After a while of waiting Shelly asked, "Do you think she's ignoring us?"

Thomas took a step back and yelled up at a second story window. "Leedee! Are you ignoring us!?"

There was no reply.

"She's most likely not home." Percy observed as he tapped his chin with his paw.

Shelly sighed. "I guess we'll have to look somewhere else."

They returned to where they had left their bicycles and started to walk them down the length of Terrace Hill. Shelly's stomach growled.

"Wow, Shelly! Do you have a monster in there?" Thomas humorously asked.

"I didn't have time for breakfast this morning. A lot of the food in the house needs to be thrown out, so I'm running on empty."

"Why do you have to throw out your food?" Percy inquired with interest.

"Because the electricity went out and most of the food spoiled."

"I had milk with my cereal today." Thomas confessed. "It was warm but it tasted okay."

Shelly scrunched her face. "Ew – That's really gross."

"I can't eat Fruity Rockets without milk, they cut the roof of my mouth." He stuck his finger into his mouth and pointed to the roof of it to better stress his point.

Thomas was really growing on her. "I generally don't eat cereal. I like eggs, toast and bacon." She pondered a moment. "I wonder how long eggs can be unrefrigerated before they spoil."

The boy shrugged his shoulders. "I like cereal, especially if it has marshmallows in it."

Shelly was about to get on her bike and suggest they ride home to get lunch, when she spied Wendy Freeman passing by on her bicycle. It wasn't hard to tell who it was; she recognized the French horn instrument case that stuck out of her rear basket.

"Wendy!" Shelly shouted and waved her hand.

It was enough to catch the attention of the girl in the grey cardigan. She pressed on her brakes and quickly looked over to where Shelly and Thomas were standing. It took her a few moments to recognize her but once she did, she turned her bike around and pedaled over to them.

Thomas picked up Percy and held him tightly in his arms.

"Hi Shelly." Wendy offered as she placed her feet on the ground to steady herself.

"How are you holding up?" Shelly asked

"Okay I guess." She shrugged. "I'm starting to miss my lessons with Mr. Dayton. Do you know if anyone's parents have turned up yet?"

"Not that I know of." Shelly confessed.

Wendy sighed and then pointed behind her. "I just came back from visiting Terrace Hill Middle School. That place is like a graveyard. It's so quiet and eerie. The playground is amazing but no one was playing on it."

"Don't you live out of town?" Shelly nodded to the far west. "Why did you come all the way over here?"

Wendy pulled her long black hair behind her ear. "I stayed with Evelynn. It was a good thing too, because when the electricity went out, it would have been very scary to be home by myself."

"I don't blame you." Shelly remembered being hungry. "Hey, you work at the corner store, right?"

"Well, yeah—sometimes, why?"

"A lot of my food spoiled and today is normally my family's grocery day. I wanted to pick up some things but the store is closed."

"I think everything is closed until the adults come back, but I wouldn't want you or anyone to starve. I know where Mr. Corrigan hides a set of keys, and I can let you in." Wendy paused for a moment. She twiddled her fingers and went through a checklist in her head. "Your mom has credit, right? I'm sure Mr. Corrigan can bill her later for anything you buy."

"That sounds okay with me. My mom always said if I needed something in an emergency that I could just charge it to her account."

"I don't think it gets any more emergency than this." Wendy laughed. "Follow me."

"Fantastic!" Shelly said with excitement. "I don't know what I would have done if you hadn't showed up. It must be our lucky day!"

Wendy snickered and muttered under her breath. "You don't know the half of it."

Shelly was in process of mounting her bike and didn't hear that last part. Meanwhile, Thomas helped Percy into his backpack and got on his bike.

"Lead the way!" Shelly exclaimed with vigor.

They rode their bikes from Terrace Hill down towards Main Street. They passed Gaines Diamond where the Applewood Cinders would play every summer. Shelly was content with passing by until Thomas yelled from behind. "Shelly wait!"

Shelly pressed hard on her brake handles, causing her tires to skid across the pavement before coming to a complete stop. Wendy heard him as well and she slowed so she could safely look behind her.

Thomas had stopped his bike and hastily set it on the ground. He ran to a spot on the grass, a short distance from a tiny tree. He then made a running leap onto something that was hidden on the ground.

"What is it, Thomas?" Shelly asked, completely confused as to what was happening.

Thomas giggled and soon he cheered. He then turned around and thrusted up his new treasure. "I found twenty dollars!" The bill flapped slightly in the breeze.

"Good job!" Percy commended from behind him.

"Wow! Way to go!" Shelly cheered. "What are the chances?"

Wendy just smiled to herself and watched patiently as the two of them wore out their enthusiasm. "That's really cool." She finally offered once Thomas returned to his bike and they caught up to her. "How did you see it?"

"I was looking for baseballs!" Thomas smiled with glee.

"Well, it's no baseball, but it's certainly something just as good. What are you going to spend it on?"

"I don't know!" He pondered as his face beamed with his newfound fortune. "Maybe candy?"

"That's a good plan!" Shelly called back to him. "Are you ready to go?"

Thomas stuffed the twenty-dollar bill in his pocket and shouted back, "Ready!"

When they arrived at Corrigan's Corner Store, Wendy noticed something fishy and stopped well before reaching the front doors. Shelly and Thomas weren't far behind her, and stopped when they saw it too. The front glass doors of the store were shattered.

"Whoa!" Shelly breathed as goose bumps traveled up her arm. It wasn't like this earlier this morning."

"It must have recently happened." Wendy voiced nervously.

"What happened?" Thomas asked with concern.

"I don't know." Shelly replied. "We should check it out."

The three of them pedaled the rest of the way to the store and planted their bikes on the sidewalk. The scattered glass reminded Shelly of when her hoop had cut into her neighbor's car.

"I guess I don't need that key after all." Shelly lightly joked as she assessed the damage.

"This is so bad. Shelly, look!" Wendy
pointed inside. The shelves were knocked
over, with packages of snacks and other food
scattered all over the ground. Shelly took
her hula-hoop off her shoulder and gripped it
tightly.

"What do you think caused this?" Wendy
asked without expecting an answer.

Shelly took a step carefully over the
threshold of the door frame and stepped
lightly on the glass, the fragments crunched
beneath her feet.

"Do you think this is a good idea?"
Thomas asked, while hesitating at the
entrance.

"Take the utmost care, Lady Shelly. There
could be brigands or worse still within."
Percy warned from over Thomas' shoulder.

Wendy's eyes widened with surprise. "Did
the rabbit just talk!?"

"Yup!" Thomas confessed cheerfully.
"Surprise!"

"Wendy, Percy. Percy, Wendy." Shelly
introduced briefly as she scoped out the
damage.

The knighted rabbit turned around to
speak to her directly. "A pleasure to make
your acquaintance, Lady Wendy."

"Ah—" Wendy hesitated. "—Okay."
Wendy tried to smile her nervousness away.
"So... what's it like being a rabbit?"

"I'm not sure, exactly. What's it like being
a human?" Percy returned with his own
curiosity.

Shelly eased her way deeper into the
store. She surveyed everything that was out
of place; it was a mess. It looked like
someone had just broken in to cause damage.

33

Someone was hungry for potato chips though, but didn't finish the entire bag. There were broken chips mixed in with all the other packages on the floor. One bag had been half eaten, crumpled up and just left on the ground. It was as if who or whatever had caused the damage had been hungry, but not enough to finish the bag.

"How could anyone want to do this?" Wendy asked after taking a moment to examine all the trouble that was caused.

A gumball machine had been smashed and its contents were everywhere. The candy aisle was the worst; chocolate wrappers were strewn across the floor, boxes were thrown, and everything was in such disarray, it made them all sad to look at it. It appeared that a lot of the candy had been taken.

Shelly's eyes kept darting between the grocery aisles, but she didn't spy anyone. It was a small store and there weren't very many places for someone to hide.

Percy's ears twitched and then stood straight up. "Pardon my interruption of your investigation, but I heard something coming from behind the building. Perhaps we should check to see who or what is causing the ruckus."

"Good idea, Percy." Thomas said with a nod.

Shelly retreated from the inside of the store, stepped carefully over the broken glass and then back to the sidewalk. She looked up and down the street and then to her left where an alley separated the corner store from Mel's Hardware Outlet.

In the alley were two girls who looked nearly identical, their dark brunette hair

framed their faces in short bobs. Had it not
been for the hoodies they wore, Shelly
wouldn't have been able to tell them apart.
One wore a blue sweatshirt with a black
heart stitched to the front; the other wore
similar, though the colors were reversed.
The hearts appeared like they were stitched
on like Frankenstein's monster's head. They
wore Terrace Hill Middle School softball caps,
and appeared to be a few years younger
than Shelly.

    There were several candy wrappers on the
ground, and one of the girls was still eating
an Atomic Chocolate Bar while the other
rested a baseball bat over her shoulders.
Two backpacks sat on the ground at their
feet, and they looked full to the brim.

RRIGAN'S
ATOMIC CHOCOLATE!
THE EXPOSLIVE CANDY WITHIN
IN STOCK!
CANDY SODA
MUTTER GUM
ATOMIC CHOCOLATE
CANDY SODA
ATOMIC CHOCOLATE!

Chapter 6

"Hey!" Shelly shouted at them. "Did you break into the store?" Shelly was mad. It was pretty clear to her that they were the ones who did it.

"Who, us?" Replied the one in the blue hoodie.

"It was like that when we got here." The other one said.

Shelly walked right up to them and pointed at the wrappers on the ground. "I bet all this candy was yours to begin with, huh? And you just so happened to eat it behind a store that was recently broken into, right?"

They both smirked. "We were hungry. We took what we needed." Said the girl with the blue hoodie.

The one in black walked between Shelly and her twin dragging a wooden baseball bat with her. She stopped a few inches from Shelly's face. "So what if it wasn't, Legs? No one was home, so we helped ourselves. Isn't that what you're doing?"

Shelly stared down the girl. Lydia was far more intimidating to her, not to mention taller. The girls appeared to be at least two years younger. "My mom has credit. It's way different than stealing."

The girl in the blue hoodie taunted her. "Ooooo – your mom has credit. Whoopty-doo. Our mom has credit too."

The girl in front of Shelly continued to smile. "So now what, Legs? Anything else you wanna say to us?"

KAT
ATOMIC CHOCOLATE!

Shelly narrowed her eyes to make sure that the girl knew she meant business. "If your mom has credit let's go write down everything you took. That way we make sure she pays for it when she comes back."

"That's not my job." The girl weaved her head like a snake. "You want to keep track so badly, YOU do it!"

"Come on, Kit!" Her sister called as she pulled her backpack of stolen goods onto her shoulders. "Legs has a lot of work to do counting candy bars. You don't want to keep her."

Kit continued to smile while she walked backwards and snagged her backpack, never taking her eyes off Shelly. After reaching where her sister stood, she stuck out her tongue before giving her sibling a high-five. The two of them laughed as they skipped down the rest of the alley before disappearing around the corner.

Thomas stood at the mouth of the alley, hugging Percy, while Wendy kept back.

"I don't know if I would have been able to say anything." Wendy replied as she tapped her shoe three times on the cement.

"I get so sick of bullies who think they can take or do whatever they want. It isn't right!" Shelly vented as she tried to unclench her fists; she hadn't noticed until now that they were balled up the entire time.

"It's too bad they were able to make off with their ill-gotten gains." Percy mentioned.

Shelly stared at the ground where all the wrappers sat. She had disappointed herself. "What else could I have done?"

Percy leapt out of Thomas' embrace. "You stood up for what you believed in, Lady

Shelly. That's nothing to be ashamed of.
You did exactly what you should have and
you made sure those kids knew what they
were doing was wrong."

"Yeah! Way to go, Shelly!" Thomas
cheered with a smile on his face. "You did a
good job." He gave her a big thumbs up.

Wendy nodded. "That was very inspiring.
We at least know who took everything and
can leave a description and an estimate of
what they took in a note for Mr. Corrigan
when he gets back. I don't think he would
have wanted anyone to get hurt because of
it. Besides, I'm sure they'll get a tummy
ache from eating all that candy."

Shelly chuckled softly, envisioning them
hunched over and complaining about their
stomachs. "It'll serve them right." She was
feeling a lot better about what happened.
"Thanks guys. And Wendy, don't sweat it,
okay? You're helping in your own way. All
of us will. And that's what matters, right?"

"Right!" Everyone said in unison.

Just then, Thomas' stomach growled.

Shelly laughed silently to herself. "It
sounds like you caught my monster. I think
it's time we found some healthier food to
take back home, what do you think?"

"Well said, Lady Shelly." Percy remarked
with encouragement.

With Thomas' backpack filled and a receipt
added to her mother's store credit, Shelly,
Thomas and Percy waved goodbye to Wendy,
then rode their bikes back to Abby's house.

Abby was reading on the porch, sitting
next to where Clarissa Betterman played
with a plastic tea set with her teddy bear. A

strand of her hair gripped the handle of her cup and another reached around and held up her teddy bear's arm to make it look as if he was holding it himself.

Ximena Martinez sat on the porch swing with her parasol opened in order to keep the sun off her neck. A flash of light poured out from around the frame of the front door and then door opened to reveal a rippling portal. Out walked Max with a box filled with cans, packages and other food stuffs. He saw Shelly as she parked her bicycle on the lawn where all the other kids had parked theirs. Max nodded to her before turning around, shutting the door, reopening it, and walking back inside the house.

Abby looked up from her book. "Hello, Sun."

Shelly smiled. "Hello, Moon." The greeting was a boost of confidence that she was missing.

Abby noticed a change had come over her best friend. "Any luck finding answers?"

Shelly sighed. "I talked to Mindy, the girl who sewed the patch for Lydia." She, Thomas and Percy walked up to the porch to join the rest of them. Shelly plopped down on a step below Abby while helping Thomas get out of his backpack. "She said that the patches can turn us into our shadow selves."

"What does that mean?" Abby asked with worry.

Shelly pointed to her arm. "You know how you get a shot and it hurts when you look at it?"

"I think so?" Abby's face scrunched up as if she could squeeze meaning out of what Shelly was trying to say.

"Well patches are like that. They are the bandage but the pain is still there. Too many patches and all you see are wounds."

Abby sighed with her confusion. "I don't think I understand what you're trying to say."

Shelly frowned. "It sounded a lot better when Mindy explained it."

Ximena spoke up, her voice was filled with a cold distance, "It's like a scar on your face. You see it every day and you're ashamed of it. One day you can't stand looking at it anymore so you cover it up with makeup. But no matter how pretty you make yourself appear, you know underneath it's still there. You're ashamed of that person in the mirror." She blinked her long eyelashes. "The shadow self is what lies beneath the makeup. It's those ugly parts that you haven't accepted about yourself. You hide those parts in the shadows until you're ready." Her face remained a haunting calm. "When you realize the scars are who you are, that there was nothing wrong with you and that you were beautiful all along - that's when you decide to take the makeup off."

Abby and Shelly stole a glance at one another wide-eyed in surprise. Ximena was always so quiet. Who would have thought she'd be so insightful? Shelly was the first to break their gaze.

"Wow Ximena... I think that describes it pretty well." Shelly blinked a few times as she tried to register some kind of emotion off Ximena's face, yet she appeared so unaffected by what she said. What Ximena said made her heart hurt.

Thomas interrupted Shelly's contemplations. "Scars are cool! Why would anyone want to cover them up?"

The Mendoza sister smirked briefly and then smoothed out a wrinkle on her dress and unfolded a bit of lace.

Max returned from inside the house and he noticed a change in everyone's moods so he was slightly hesitant to ask. "Hey Abby? There's this kid in your kitchen wanting to know if you have any ketchup."

Abby stood up and folded her book under her arm. "I think we have some... maybe in the pantry? I'll show them."

"Who is it?" Shelly asked with curiosity, happy that she had something to distract her from what Ximena had brought to light. It also wasn't every day that Abby had other kids over.

Max shrugged his shoulders. "Beats me. I've never seen him before."

Chapter 7

Shelly stood up and then followed Abby as she went inside. "You have a stranger in your house?"

Abby shrugged as she put her book down on a shelf. "I don't know. There's been a lot of kids wanting peanut butter and jelly sandwiches. I just sat down not long ago. I ran out of bread."

"That's a lot of sandwiches." Shelly expressed with gaping wide eyes. Maybe leaving Abby alone with all these other kids was a bad idea. She should have stuck around to help – if not eat. She was famished and so was Thomas.

When they reached the kitchen, they found Gan sitting at the table with Jasmine. They both had plates in front of them as well as a knife and a fork in their hands, waiting to be served.

The whole place smelled of french fries, and Shelly noticed it was because there was a giant pile of them on a cookie sheet near the oven. A frying pan sat on the stove with a few more fries cooking in it. Shelly found it a bit odd, as she was used to baking them in the oven.

A boy walked out of the pantry with a bottle of ketchup in his hands. His hoodie matched the color of the bottle. He also wore jeans and brown sneakers. His cheeks were as round as his stomach and his shoulders were sloped. He meandered back over to the skillet where he scooped up some fries with a spatula and placed them onto the pile.

"I see you found the ketchup." Abby announced.

The kid was big; probably a grade or more ahead of them. His complexion was as striking as Shelly's. He turned around with the ketchup bottle in hand and displayed it like a commercial. His smile ran into his cheeks, "Yes I did!"

"What are you doing?" Shelly asked.

He held out the spatula before him like a sword. "I'm on the important quest of making french fries – but, more importantly, fry sauce!"

His enthusiasm was contagious and Shelly couldn't help but snort out of her nose at his dramatic display.

"And who are you?" Abby inquired while trying to keep a straight face.

He opened his arms and cheerfully repeated himself. "Frysauce!"

"No – your name? What is your name?"

He motioned with his hands to show separation between his words. "Fry. Sauce." And then he brought his hands together. "Frysauce."

"Your name is Frysauce and you're going to make fry sauce?" Shelly asked with a chuckle.

"That's right! You got it!" He laughed. "I'm named after what I love and I love fry sauce. Mmm. Mmm. Mmm. And who are you?"

"My name is Shelly Wynn."

"Shelly Wynn, huh? I should call you Fireshoes, but you look more like a Shelly to me."

He piqued her interest. "You saw the race, huh?"

"Yes-I-did." He replied quickly. "I don't know about you, but if that was me, I'd let the car eater win. Then again, my shoes don't catch fire like yours do. Oh – speaking of fire."

He turned around, set the ketchup on the counter and transferred the remaining fries from the pan onto the cookie sheet. He then shut off the burner and watched as the fire went out.

"There's no way that I would let Lydia Gaines have the satisfaction of beating me." Shelly affirmed.

"Okay, okay. No worries here. You do you." He poured some ketchup into a bowl where other ingredients waited. He mixed them all together with a whisk. "And I'll do me. Let me introduce you all to a secret that has been handed down from mother to son. I give you – 'Frysauce's Fry Sauce'."

He placed the bowl in the middle of the table, setting the tray of fries next to it as though they were a side dish. Jasmine and Gan were quick to grab some French fries, but Abby was the first to try the sauce.

Frysauce patted his stomach like a drum. "And the award for the most adventurous goes to..."

Abby smiled and then swallowed. The taste made her mouth tingle. She could have sworn there was mayonnaise and maybe taco powder – but she wasn't exactly sure. "Abby," she finished Frysauce's sentence as she chewed.

"Is this not the best fry sauce you've ever tasted?!" He asked with a squeak in his

voice.

"It's the only fry sauce that I've tasted and it's good." The satisfied bookworm grabbed another fry.

"Yesssssss! She loves it! Fry sauce for everyone." He grabbed a bunch of fries and slathered a generous portion of fry sauce onto them before shoving them in his mouth at the same time.

"Give me one moment." Shelly excused herself as she tried to stifle her laughter at the ridiculousness of it all. She rushed to the front door where all the other kids were hanging out. "Anyone want any french fries with some special fry sauce?"

Shelly sat on the porch with everyone after they'd finishing eating. She couldn't remember the last time she had eaten so many fries. Abby was sipping a glass of water.

Frysauce marveled at all the satisfied stomachs. "Anyone want any more fries? I could go make some more."

"Noooo..." Abby groaned. "No more fries."

Thomas giggled. "You shouldn't have eaten so many, Abby."

"They were so good though." Jasmine chimed in as she played with a bubble in her hand.

Frysauce appeared more than content with everyone's answer.

"So what are we going to do next, Shell?" Her best friend asked as she let go of her glass and made it float in the air.

"We need to find Lydia and make sure that she's okay. Bully or not, if the patches are

doing something horrible to her, she needs
our help." Shelly was determined. She
didn't want to give up simply because Lydia
was a pain in the neck. "Who wants to
help?" She cast her eyes across everyone's
face.

"Javier and I will." Ximena volunteered.

Her brother huffed. "Come on, Ximena!
Call me Max!"

"No." Her face remained calm and
unconcerned with his disapproval.

"Okay – fine..." He relented. "We'll talk
about it later." Max insisted as he leaned
against the house.

Jasmine raised her hand. "I'm in."

"Me too!" Gan announced as he turned his
baseball cap to the side.

Clarissa whispered into her teddy bear's
ear and then asked, "What do you think, Mr.
Cuddles?" She leaned her ear near her
bear's mouth, then nodded. "Mr. Cuddles
wants to help, and I should make sure that
he doesn't get into trouble."

Frysauce raised an eyebrow. "Does your
bear get into a lot of trouble?"

"Oh, no..." She blinked apologetically.
"Only when he gets caught."

"You're serious?" Frysauce questioned
with a slack jaw.

Percy jested. "He does have the look of a
bandit."

"Mostly though he just sleeps." Clarissa
reassured everyone.

Max muttered beneath his breath. "El
bandito de la siesta."

Thomas raised his hand. "Percy and I will
help. You can count on us!"

"Quite right, Thomas." Percy affirmed.

"What about you, Frysauce? You want to help?" Abby asked after noticing he hadn't given a pledge one way or the other.

"So... are we playing a city-wide game of hide and go seek?" He asked as he scratched his belly. "Or maybe we could pretend like we're hunting for Bigfoot."

Ximena tilted her head. "Does Lydia have big feet? I didn't notice." She tried to keep a dead pan face but the corners of her mouth crept upwards into a half grin.

"We're not pretending that she's Bigfoot, guys." Abby softly demanded. She noticed that she was nervously playing with her braid, and stopped abruptly, taking another drink of water. After she finished she asked, "Thomas, is there anywhere Lydia likes to go?"

Thomas thought for a little while. "We used to go to the museum, the baseball diamond, Pouche Park and the Lilly Gardens."

Shelly thought back to what Wendy had said about most places being closed. "She's probably not at the museum, the diamond or the Gardens since most of those aren't open. You don't think she went all the way to Pouche Park, do you?"

Abby shook her head. "I doubt it. It would take forever to get there, even if we rode our bikes." She pondered. "But there is Willow Park, and there are all the school's playgrounds. Maybe she went to one of those places?"

Frysauce folded his arms in front of him. "Well, we wouldn't all be able to walk to those places together. We don't want to be out past dark. There are monsters out there."

"You mean like more kids turning eighteen and losing their minds?" Abby asked, plucking her glass of water out of the air as if she feared it would fall.

The boy shook his head. "I'm talking about monsters. Like real monsters! The kind with skull faces, blue fur and sharp teeth." He unfolded his arms and pretended his hands had claws. "I've seen them! They only come out at night and you're only safe if you have enough light to scare them away."

Clarissa and Thomas both pulled their stuffed animals close to them. Abby brought her knees to her chest and Jasmine popped her bubble. Max, Gan and Ximena all leaned in to hear more.

"I'm telling you, you don't want to be out after dark." Frysauce reaffirmed with a small quiver in his voice.

Shelly stood up with conviction. "Even more reason for us to find her, before something else does."

Chapter 8

"Okay everyone! Lydia needs our help."
Shelly rallied as she straddled her bicycle.
Everyone was ready to search the
neighborhood. "Something funky is
happening with her patches. That could
happen to anyone of us. She might be mean
sometimes, but she's also Thomas' cousin
and she means a lot to him. She's the only
family he has left." Shelly expounded
further.

"Well said, Lady Shelly!" Percy cheered
from Thomas' front basket.

Shelly nodded to each leader. "Ximena –
you take Max, Clarissa and Mr. Cuddles to
check out Willow Park and anything along
the way. Frysauce? You take Jasmin and Gan
and look around the school playgrounds.
Abby, Thomas, Percy and I will check out
Pouche Park."

Abby jumped in to help relieve some of
her own fears. "Does everyone have their
flashlights? Have you made sure they work?"

Shelly turned hers on and off just to be
certain, then placed it in her backpack and
paid attention to ensure everybody else did
the same.

"Everyone meet back here before dark,
okay? If everyone isn't back in time, don't
wait up. Get somewhere safe and make sure
you have some lights like candles, lanterns
or flashlights to keep the monsters away.
Got it? And if you find Lydia, make sure
she's safe and knows about the monsters.
Try to convince her to come back with you if
you can." Shelly exhaled. "If you see a

monster, run away as fast as you can. If you can't outrun it, then hide somewhere where it can't find you."

"You don't have to tell me twice." Frysauce expressed with a frown. "I'll be on the other end of the block before it can even blink."

"I have a door memorized, just like I did with that car this morning. If there's trouble, Javier can get us out." Ximena reassured.

"Take care of each other out there and be safe." Abby warmly insisted.

All the other kids rode off. Clarissa was momentarily confused about who she was supposed to follow, making a single circle before pedaling off to catch up with Ximena and Max.

Jasmine called back enthusiastically. "Don't worry! We'll find her."

Shelly took a moment and confided in her best friend. "I like them."

Abby laughed. "I do too. I don't know what kept us from talking to any of them before."

Shelly shrugged. "A lot of things are different now."

Abby sighed. "Let's hope not for too much longer. I'm starting to miss my teachers."

"You would!" Shelly teased.

"What? I had great relationships with my teachers. I like learning things and there aren't any monsters to worry about." Abby spied across the block, looking down the street and over at the bushes just to be safe.

Shelly placed her hand on Abby's shoulder. "Hey... it'll be okay. We're a team."

53

"The best team ever!" Thomas shouted with excitement.

Abby's worries melted off her face and they were replaced with a smile. "You're right. We can do this."

Shelly nodded in agreement and turned her bike towards Pouche Park.

The ride there was a desolate one. Not a child could be seen, which came across as very weird to her. *Probably because it wasn't going to be long before the sun set.* She was glad, the fact that there could be monster wandering the street was enough to raise the hairs on the back of her neck. Seeing how quickly Abby was snatched by Alex was enough to haunt her through senior year of high school.

As Shelly tried to get the events of last night out of her head, she spotted a couple of familiar faces running along the sidewalk kicking over city trash cans. Two girls, one with a blue hoodie and a black heart and one with a black hoodie and a blue heart.

These two again? Shelly thought. The fact that they were still breaking things that didn't belong to them made her upset. *Didn't their parents teach them about respect for other people's things?* She wanted to tell them to knock it off, but she was afraid she'd get into another disagreement and she didn't have time for that. Though, despite their awful behavior, Shelly felt she needed to at least warn them of the monsters.

Shelly turned to Abby who was already watching the twins' path of destruction, aghast. "Keep heading towards the park, okay? I'm going to warn them to get inside before it gets dark."

Abby bit her lip. "Okay, be careful. If those are the same girls you told me about during lunch, they aren't the best kids in the world."

"I'll be quick. Besides, they couldn't catch me even if they tried." She gave Abby a reassuring wink before steering her bike towards them."

Kit, the girl wearing the black hoodie, ran up to another trash can and swung her baseball bat as hard as she could. It hit with a loud bang and sent the contents of the trash can spilling onto the ground. They both laughed with delight as the can roll down the sidewalk.

"Good one, Sis!" Kat roared.

"Hey!" Shelly shouted from her bike to get their attention.

"Ugh!" Kit pretended to vomit. "It's Legs again."

Her sister grabbed her hand and dragged her around the corner giggling.

Shelly groaned with irritation. *I should just let them stay after dark so they can be scared out of their minds when a monster comes after them.* The events from last night echoed in her mind and it caused her heart to skip a beat. *Just say what you need to say and leave.* She reassured herself.

Riding after them, Shelly was determined to deliver her warning. As soon as she rounded the corner she saw them standing not too far away, clapping out a song between the both of them.

"Shelly, Shelly, Shelly Wynn. Lost her hoop in a fight again. Tell her mom. Tell her

dad. She hurt a boy and now he's dead. 1...
2... 3... 4... His body fell onto the floor." The
girls grinned at her but kept their
concentration on their clapping.

Shelly was taken aback. Her face flushed
and she felt petrified. A heavy knot settled
in her chest. Shelly's mind raced with
thoughts on how they had learned her name
and how they knew about Alex.

"Hey!" Shelly repeated as she tried to
swallow some of the nervousness that
plagued her. "You need to get inside before
it's dark."

"What?" Kat yelled. "We can't hear you!"
She continued to clap her hands with her
sister.

Shelly was pretty sure that they had heard
her just fine. "I said, you need to get inside
before it is dark!" She shouted.

"Huh?" Screamed the other sister. "You'll
have to come closer!"

Now Shelly was convinced that they were
doing this just to annoy her. She took a
huge breath to help alleviate some of the
irritation, and rode her bike up so that she
was no more than a few feet away.

"I SAID, you need to go inside before it
gets DARK. There are MONSTERS!"

The girls stopped clapping and kept their
malicious smiles pasted to their faces. Kat
rushed over to Shelly and grabbed the
handles of her bike.

"Yup! We're the monsters! Tag! You're
it!" With incredible force, Kat tilted Shelly's
bicycle towards the ground, causing Shelly to
spill onto the cement. Her hoop rolled off
her shoulders and several feet away.

Everything happened so quickly, and Shelly had no time to react. Before she could even stand up, Kit grabbed her by the straps of her backpack and lifted her straight up off the ground. Shelly saw Kat hoist her bike over her head and tossed it a good distance down the street.

They are smaller than me. How are they this strong? She marveled with dread.

"Boo hoo hoo – there's monsters!" Kit taunted.

Kat jumped up and down from the surge of her strength, just dying to rid herself of the energy. "I love this!" She screamed.

Shelly struggled, trying to pry Kit's hand off of her, but her grip was tight.

"Put me down!" She finally demanded.

"I have a great idea, Sis!" Kit announced ecstatically as she maintained her hold on Shelly. "Why don't you give Legs here a few whacks and see if candy falls out. That'll teach her to stay out of our business."

"No-no-no! Don't! I was just trying to warn you!" Shelly desperately tried to explain.

Kat picked up her baseball bat. She gave it a few good practice swings in the air. The whoosh caused Shelly to cringe.

"How many do you think it'll take? Two? Three?" Kit horribly inquired.

A loud boom caused their hearts to skip a beat, enough that Kat dropped her bat and Kit loosened her grip on Shelly.

They all looked down the street just in time to see a kid with bright neon green hair, rollerblades and a jump rope blaze towards them like a rocket.

"Who the URK—"

KAT
KIT

The skater stuck out their arm and caught Kat right in the chest, knocking her to the ground.

Kit dropped Shelly and ran over to see if her sister was okay. Once she was certain, she helped Kat back to her feet.

Shelly didn't waste any time to sort out the chaos, she ran to where her hoop had rolled to, seized it in a single swoop of her hand, planted her feet and twirled it as fast as she could.

The skater spun around on their blades, swung their jump rope in the air and cracked it on the ground. A small explosion rocked the street.

"You want to fight someone?!" The kid shouted. "Fight me!!!"

Kat, now brought to her feet, grabbed her bat, pushed past her sister and pointed at the kid with the neon green hair. "I'll take your dumb head off!" She gritted her teeth and raised her bat high into the air as if she was getting ready to swing for the fences.

Shelly's hoop burned bright. The heat rolled off it with each twirl, and soon it was as bright as the headlight of a car.

Kit tugged on her sister's hoodie. The power radiating from Shelly's hoop made her cringe. "Um... Kat..."

"What?!" Kat growled back.

With a battle cry, Shelly charged at them. In a single blinding flash of blue light, Shelly's hoop sliced through the baseball bat, leaving the handle smoldering in Kat's hands.

The twins glanced at one another, then bolted down the street in terror.

Shelly was breathing heavily. She watched with satisfaction as they disappeared down the street.

The kid with the neon green hair rolled up their jump rope and then skated up to Shelly. "Are you okay?" They asked, voicing concern with a low, yet strangely melodic, tone. Their emerald green eyes shown with the light from Shelly's hoop, almost matching the green hair that swooped down over one eye. A black studded collar and matching wrist cuffs gave the stranger an intimidating look, which didn't seem to match the concern they were showing Shelly.

Shelly let the glow die off her hoop before she checked herself for injuries. "A few scrapes and maybe a bruise here and there, but I think I'll be okay." She looked the skater in the face. "Thanks for coming to my rescue..." There was something unusual about the kid, they appeared Native American, and despite all their beautiful features, Shelly couldn't quite put her finger on it.

"My name is Quinn Kiowa. You shouldn't be out much longer. I heard there are monsters in Applewood."

Shelly chuckled. "That's why I'm out here. I'm looking for someone. I want to make sure that they are safe."

Quinn nodded in the direction the twins took off in. "I hope it wasn't those two."

"No, I'm looking for Lydia Gaines."

"Oh." Quinn's expression sunk with their voice.

"No-no, it's not like that. Her patches are doing something bad to her, plus she just lost her older brother. We want to make sure she's safe."

"Oh." Quinn's tone picked up with renewed sentiment.

"You know Lydia, I take it?"

"Of course I know her."

"Really?" Shelly raised her eyebrow and then she remembered her manners. "I'm sorry, my name is Shelly Wynn."

Quinn smiled. "I know. You're on the track team for Applewood Middle School."

Shelly was now beyond confused. *First the twins and now her? What is going on.* "How do you...?"

"I've watched you practice." They chuckled. "We've shared Terrace Hills track together."

A smirk flashed across Shelly's face. "I think I would have remembered a girl with green hair."

Quinn's cheeks flushed and they let out a laugh. "I'm not a girl."

Her confusion only grew. She blinked a few times, tilted her head one way and then the next. Still perplexed she asked, "You're... a boy?"

Quinn shook her head patiently. "I'm together."

Chapter 9

Shelly pedaled as quickly as she could without leaving Quinn in the dust. Despite Shelly's ability to add her super speed to her bicycle, Quinn was able to keep a decent pace due by whipping their jump rope on the ground, using the explosion to propel them forward like a jet.

"So how does your patch work, exactly?" Quinn asked between the booms that issued from their rope.

Shelly's feet glowed softly from her pedaling. "I'm not sure exactly." She shouted back. "I think it has something to do with moving. How about yours?"

"It's only when I hit things like fingers or clapping. It also extends to whatever I'm holding so—" Quinn avoided a piece of loose cement before continuing. "It also works sometimes when I fall and hit the ground too hard."

Shelly imagined Quinn tripping on a crack in the sidewalk, falling and then being rocketed into space by a huge explosion. She laughed through her nose. Shelly was about to ask if Quinn had found that out that hard way but she spied Abby, Thomas and Percy at the entrance to the park.

Abby waved to them and shouted, "Hey! What took you so long?"

Shelly braked once she reached them and put the kickstand down with her foot. Her eyes rolled with frustration. "Ugh – I tried to warn those two and they just jumped me."

"Oh my gosh, are you okay!?" Abby ran over to her to make sure there wasn't any damage.

"Just a little roughed up."

Quinn caught up and stopped next to Shelly.

"Abby, this is—"

"Quinn!" Abby shrieked as she ran up and hugged them. Her jaw dropped, and she held Quinn at arm's length to get a good look; eyes wide. "This. Is. AMAZING! When did this happen?" She looked the skater up and down.

Shelly's eyebrow raised. "—and you two know each other?"

"Yeah – I mean – we've met a couple of times in the stands while you raced but never like THIS." She gestured to everything that Quinn was wearing.

Thomas' face was stone sober. It looked like something had gotten stuck inside his head and he stared.

Quinn blushed and looked down at the rollerblades on their feet. "I did it yesterday."

"I love it so much!" Abby clenched her fists together and held them over her heart.

Shelly watched as Quinn shrank in size. "Please stop." They muttered as they tried to hide their cheeks behind their hands.

"Thomas?" Percy asked as he touched his child's hand with his paw. "Are you, all right?"

Thomas narrowed his eyes. "I'm really confused by Quinn."

Shelly and Abby looked between him and Quinn.

"I was confused too, Thomas. Quinn is—"

"Why is your hair green?" Thomas demanded.

Quinn and Abby burst into laughter. "Most of it is a wig. The rest, I dyed." Quinn replied once they were able to contain their giggles.

"Ooooooooh—" Thomas drew out as his face returned to his cheery self. "I thought you may have been born that way like some kind of space mutant." He chuckled.

"No, I wasn't born with green hair." They shook their head with emphasis.

"I want to have blue hair!" Thomas gleefully remarked as he ran a hand through his own hair.

"Well... you may need to ask—" Shelly was interrupted by Quinn.

"You can have any color hair you want to! It's your hair. It's your decision."

Thomas threw his hands in the air out of excitement. "All right!"

Shelly thought about it. There was a time she had asked her parents to allow her to dye her hair lavender but they refused. They told her that it wasn't professional. Personally, she never understood why she couldn't. *What did it matter what other people thought? It's not their hair.* "Sure!" She concluded. "It's your hair."

"I think you'd look great with blue hair." Abby encouraged with a grin.

"I'm Thomas." He thumbed to himself and then directed his hand to his rabbit. "And this is Percy."

The rabbit bowed. "A pleasure to meet your acquaintance, Lidt Quinn."

"Lidt?" Abby asked with uncertainty.

"Of course! It's a proper title for those being both Lady and Lord. It's a rabbit title, but I think it would fit here perfectly."

The horizon stole Shelly's attention as the sun was already beginning to set. "I don't know how much time we have left. We'll split up, okay?" Shelly pointed to a statue of Laliz Pouche that was not far from the main entrance. "Abby, you Thomas and Percy take the right side of the park. Quinn and I will take the left."

"Search quickly everyone!" Quinn suggested with concern. "We have to be inside before dark." They eased down to the curb and started taking off their rollerblades.

"Come on, Thomas!" Abby cheered with enthusiasm. "I bet I'll find Lydia before you will."

"I don't think so!" Thomas retorted with glee as he chased after her into the park with Percy in tow.

"Go on in." Quinn recommended as they fiddled with the straps. "I'll catch up."

Shelly nodded and walked into the park. The pathways were all brick, lined with many flowers in well-tended beds. There were countless trees that she could climb, and several different statues that stuck out like giant mushrooms.

The statue of Laliz Pounche, an old science fiction writer who lived in Applewood many years ago, was made of bronze. It stood on a pedestal that was as tall as Shelly's hips. The statue was life-size. Laliz held a book in one hand and her glasses in the other. A plaque beneath it read: "Dream beneath the candlelight of your soul." Shelly didn't know what that meant, but it sounded pretty.

Shelly hadn't moved that far into the park before Quinn joined her.

"I hope we can find your rival." Quinn looked around, doing their best to find any trace of Lydia before nodding at Shelly.

Together, they began their search down the left path which passed through a blooming rose garden, Shelly wondered who would take care of them now that the grown-ups were gone. The park was always well-maintained; she feared what it would look like after a couple of weeks with no one to weed it.

"It's always weird taking off my rollerblades. It's like I'm stuck between wanting to glide and knowing that it won't take me anywhere. Have you ever felt that

way about something?" Quinn asked
seemingly out of nowhere as they scuffed
their shoe against the bricks.

"I feel like I should be taller after I take
off my pointe shoes. Does that count?"

"You dance ballet?" Quinn asked, starry-
eyed. "I've always wanted to take classes.
Are you any good?"

"You should learn. My teacher was always
looking for bo—other students." Shelly felt
embarrassed about the slip up, like she'd
almost given the wrong answer in class. *It
certainly will take some time to get used to
not using 'girl' or 'boy'.* "And yeah... I'm
pretty good. I just do it for fun. There's a
girl in my class, Cadence, she's trying to
make it her life. I just don't have that
dedication. I like too many things and that's
all she does."

Quinn winked. "I know what you mean."

Shelly spied every which way hoping that
she could spot Lydia's blonde curls and then
remembered the nature of Alex's patch.

"I really hope that Lydia hasn't eaten
something where we wouldn't be able to
recognize her."

Her search partner blinked a few times to
understand what she meant. "Lydia can eat
things and something changes to her
appearance?"

"Yea – like earlier, she turned into a car so
that she could race me."

Quinn's shoulders sank. "She ate a car?"

Shelly nodded. "Swallowed it whole."

"Things are so weird right now." They
attempted to recover their posture.

"We're trying to find a girl who bullied me
for the most of my life to make sure that

her patches, which are stitched onto her soul, aren't hurting her and praying that a monster hasn't already devoured her. Nothing is normal."

"Hey, speaking of normal, is that her over there?" Quinn gestured with their hand, directing Shelly's attention to a small bridge that crossed over a churning brook. Lydia sat in the middle of the bridge at the edge looking down at the water.

Chapter 10

Shelly's heart skipped with a sense of relief, while her stomach rampaged with butterflies. She could only imagine how Lydia was going to react to her being here. As she had to do with all the other times she had interacted with her. Shelly took a deep breath and rushed to where the path met the mouth of the bridge.

"Lydia!" She called out.

The isolated Lydia Gaines turned her head to reveal puffy eyes. Several tears still streamed down her face. She sniffed and tried to wipe away the evidence of her emotions. "Leave me alone." Her voice was small, and her head ducked down, like a turtle retreating into its shell.

Shelly pushed past the want to escape the conversation. "Thomas is worried about you. I'm worried about you."

Lydia narrowed her eyes as her face flashed with anger. "You don't know anything about me – I'm fine! I can take care of myself." She stood up and brushed the dirt off of her clothes.

"I'm sure you can – but we need to get inside. It's not safe out here."

"No one is safe around you, Whinny." The grass-stained girl sneered before storming off the opposite side of the bridge and towards another path that lead to the entrance of the park.

Mindy had warned her about this; on how Lydia would likely not want her help. Had the circumstances been different, she would have walked away. However, Thomas was

counting on her.

"You're definitely rivals." Quinn observed. "This isn't as hopeful as I thought it would be."

"She's not thinking straight." Shelly said more for her own benefit than Quinn's. "Lydia! Wait up!" Shelly yelled after as she jogged to catch up.

"I said, 'Leave me alone'!" Lydia barked as she clenched her fists. She found a place in the brook where she could walk across the rocks as a short cut.

"I talked with Mindy at the SOK Market. She told me that your patches may be too much for you right now." She swallowed as she jumped the brook to catch up. "I'm trying to help."

"I don't want your help! I don't want anyone's help. I don't need you." Another tear streamed down her face. Lydia didn't bother to wipe it away. Her voice cracked. "I don't need anyone."

"You don't mean that. Your patches are making you say these things."

"My patches?! You think it's all about my patches? My parents were never there for me. They were always too busy with Alex."

Lydia stopped at the base of the statue of Laliz Pouche and screamed up at her, "Well who needs you?!" Her lips quivered and more tears flooded onto her cheeks. "And now he's gone!" She kicked at some bricks in the path repeatedly. "He's gone! He's gone! He's gone! And it's your fault!" She pointed at Shelly. "You took him away."

"Alex was a monster, Lydia. He was going to—"

"He was my brother! He was the only one there for me." She was breathing heavily, as if the words she spoke exhausted her, and the oxygen she was pulling in just wasn't enough. Lydia grabbed a brick that had come loose and she swallowed it as she cried. Her skin turned rough and red; her hair and clothes melded to her like a statue's. Shelly notice the groves between the edges of her brick-like exterior, and how they had filled with mortar.

"This is all I have!" She struck herself in the chest with her fist and her chest cracked. Flakes of brick and dust fell onto the path beneath her. "You took him away." Lydia choked and her new skin danced about her, shifting between her usual white pigment and red. She put her hand over her mouth and quickly turned away. She spat the brick back up and it thudded harmlessly to the ground.

Shelly's guilt bubbled up into her throat. "I'm sorry, Lydia." She thought back to that night; the moment she'd cut Alex in half, when Abby was screaming for her life and how terrified they all were. *No! She's not dragging me with her.*

Shelly had saved Abby. Lydia *wanted* her to end her brother. What had Lydia said? Something about how her brother couldn't get the story straight? Was the same thing happening to Lydia? Could she not remember what happened?

Something else rose up inside her. "You know what? No! I understand you're upset about losing your brother. No one can expect you to get over that in a day – and who is to say you ever will? But your

brother was the one who was dangerous –
not me! He was going to eat Abby – or did
you forget that part? He was out of
control." Shelly wasn't sure how any of this
sounded, but she felt it needed to be said.
"What if he had escaped the house? How
many other kids would have been hurt or
worse? Is that something Alex – the real
Alex – would have wanted? How would you
have felt, knowing that we could have
stopped him and didn't? You may be mean a
lot of the time, but I know you wouldn't want
that. Despite your insults and horribleness,
deep down, I know you want to be a good
person."

Quinn had stopped few feet away from
them, giving the two of them space to work
through their problems. The green-haired
skater was flabbergasted, but also impressed
with how Shelly was handling things.

Lydia wasn't angry anymore. Her eyes
searched back and forth, looking to one side
to the next, as if searching for something in
her mind. She frowned, lips quivering. She
buried her face in her hands and bawled. Her
knees buckled and she fell to the ground,
losing herself in all her tears.

"I'm not a good person." She wailed
behind her fingers. "No one wants me
around. I'm too horrible. I'm just not a good
person. I'll never be a good person."

Shelly and Quinn both felt sympathy,
welled up, and couldn't help but cry for her.
Lydia's pain had touched something inside
them; a reminder of what they'd heard
whispered in the darkest part of their minds.
While Shelly debated what she should do,
Quinn rushed over to Lydia's side, and

73

wrapped the girl in a tight hug.

Taking Quinn's hug as the right course, Shelly wanted nothing more than to share in that moment of vulnerability, where all defenses had finally collapsed, and to help relieve all those years of torture. Shelly took a step forward—but a distant screech caused the hair on Shelly's arms to stand on end. Her heart thudded heavily in her chest and she looked up at the sky to see where the noise had come from. Blinking a few times, she wiped away the tears so she could see clearly. The sky was filled with shadows. It made her nervous. Shelly removed the hula hoop off her shoulder and moved closer to her friends.

"Guys? Did you hear that?"

Quinn and Lydia didn't notice the sound or heard what Shelly was asking.

Hoop in hand Shelly scanned the area, checking the gardens, pathways, benches and statues for any sign of something out of the ordinary or that could have made that noise. She hoped that Abby, Thomas or Percy were fooling around, but she knew it was far outside their character.

Then, right when Shelly was about to dismiss it, she heard it again. This time it was louder – a nightmarish screech that came from overhead. Shelly spied the source of the noise hovering in the sky.

It swooped down and landed directly atop the statue of Laliz Pouche. With a heavy landing, it's talon-like feet gripped Laliz's head as if it were a familiar perch. The creature was a giant eyeball the size of a beach ball with two arms fit with a single claw at each end; its skin was green and

tight against its bones. As it whipped its
barbed tail in the air, it stretched its bat-like
wings until its tail settled around the
statue's neck.

Shelly was petrified as the one-eyed
monster stared directly at her. The one
giant pupil glowed like fire, then winked out
as the eye split into a giant mouth with
hundreds of sharp teeth. The horror roared
out into the coming night, signaling all to its
prey.

Chapter 11

Quinn was startled. They released Lydia and fell onto their back fitted in terror as they saw the beast. "Holy buckets – what is that!?"

Its mouth snapped shut and turned its crimson gaze on Quinn and the still sobbing Lydia.

"Both of you, MOVE!" Shelly cried out as the abomination unfolded its wings and prepared to pounce.

Quinn crawled backwards like a crab in order to better get their footing, but Lydia refused to budge.

Knowing Lydia was only moments away from becoming monster chow, Shelly stepped between Lydia and the statue, spinning her hula hoop above her head.

The monster opened its mouth wide; drool seeped between its teeth. Hissing ferociously, it leapt towards Shelly. Shelly held her breath and quickly jammed her glowing hoop inside the monster's mouth, enough to lodge it open. The heat seared the creature's tongue and it roared with pain.

It thrashed its head back and forth, and Shelly struggled to hold onto her hoop. "LYDIA RUN!!!" She screamed.

"Just let it eat me..." Lydia begged as she sunk farther to the bricks.

"WHAT?!" Shelly demanded as her fear seeped into her bones.

The monster flapped its wings rapidly and drew itself into the air. It flew backwards, with its tail lashing out and then wrapped around Shelly's waist. It squeezed her

tightly, and Shelly felt her insides being pressed together. She couldn't breathe. With a yank, the tail pulled Shelly away from the monster's mouth. In little time, the monster dislodged the hula hoop and it tossed Shelly like she was a piece of wadded up paper. Shelly slammed into the ground; the air rushed out of her lungs, leaving her temporarily breathless.

Quinn was up on their feet and charged at the eye-thing angrily. "Nothing messes with my friends!" With a quick flick of their hand, the jump rope unfurled and was launched into the air. It snapped against the horror, the resulting explosion cased it lurch to one side as the boom echoed through the park.

The monster keened. It turned on Quinn, its mouth shut and the reddish glow burned brighter. A hum built in creature's head and the beast expelled a rippling haze that flooded over Quinn, causing them to stagger backwards.

For Quinn, the world shifted and everything wavered. They felt nauseous, and had difficulties determining which way was left or right. Everything was spinning.

"Quinn!" Shelly yelled out as she struggled to get back to her feet. She snatched her hoop from off the ground and spun it around her arms and then twisted it to rebuild its glow.

The monster recognized that the child had fallen beneath its spell and it threw up its tail, like a scorpion, ready to strike.

They all heard a familiar voice call out. "Up!"

A brown rabbit with a wooden sword flew through the air and landed squarely on one of the monster's wing.

The creature was stunned, giving Percy enough time to raise his sword high above his head and cry out, "You're grounded," before slamming the wooden blade against the monster's wing.

The abomination wailed as it tumbled to the ground. Percy jumped from the creature's wing and rolled a short distance away, hopping back up into a fighting position.

"Nice throw, Thomas!" Abby cheered as the two of them ran into view.

Thomas laughed. "Thanks! And good job Percy!"

The creature flailed on the ground, growling and snapping its teeth at the air around it until such a time it could stand back up.

Quinn tried to get their bearings. They kept seeing double, sometimes triple. Everything kept twirling, much like Shelly's hoop. Still clutching their jump rope, Quinn pulled it back and snapped it at the beast. The rope fell short and lifelessly fell to the ground without as much as a whisper. They stumbled and tried to keep themselves from falling over.

Shelly rushed back into the fray. She brought her blazing hoop down overtop its head, but the monster jumped out of the way. Shelly tried to slash at it, but the creature was too quick.

With a flick of its tail, it snagged Shelly's ankle, and her foot was pulled out from under her. She tumbled to the ground and her hoop dimmed after losing its motion.

    The eye-beast gripped the ground with its
claws and then hoisted Shelly off the grass
by her foot and tossed her into Percy. The
two of them smacked into one another and
rolled into a heap.
    Abby looked for something to throw but
couldn't find anything in range.
    The horror's giant eye settled on Lydia.
She was still sobbing, completely ignoring
the fight around her. The creature opened
its maw and drool dripped off its teeth,
pooling on the ground like slime.
    "Look out, Lydia!" Abby called out.
    "Don't give up, Leedee!" Thomas shouted.
    Lydia lifted her head and stared directly
into the monster's eye and saw Alex in that
hellish glow. Alex had meant everything to
her and she remembered the moment she
saw his personality, his charm and his wit all
disappear into that terrifying light.
    The beast rolled its tongue out of its
mouth and charged her. It raised its claws
high above its eye. As it neared her, the
monster opened its mouth wider in order to
devour her whole.
    "LEEDEE!" Thomas screamed.
    Percy grabbed his sword and tried to put
himself between them, but knew that he
would reach them too late. Quinn could
barely stand. Shelly's hoop was no longer
glowing. Abby couldn't look away from the
scene before her.
    Lydia's face flushed with anger, her eyes
awash with a bright light. She held up her
hand and screamed, "LEAVE ME ALONE!"
    The light in her eyes also poured from her
hand, covering the monster as if it were fire.
It filled the whole park, briefly blinding all of

the children. The creature didn't even have time to wail as its eye, flesh and bones dissolved into tiny pieces of paper.

When the light finally dissolved, all that remained was a glowing badge hovering in the air, no bigger than a silver dollar. It was much like the one Alex had left behind, but this one was smaller. The pieces of paper swirled up into the air before burning up; their ashes carried off by a breeze.

Lydia slowly stood up and plucked it from the air. She held it in her hand and inspected it briefly.

Quinn fell to the ground in order to take a moment to rest. The sensation was like they had rolled down a steep hill. As the seconds trudged on, the world stopped shifting and Quinn started to feel better.

Thomas ran up to Lydia and gave her a giant hug. "Leedee, are you okay?"

Lydia tore her eyes from the badge that was still resting in her hand, and tiredly looked at Thomas, as though even that small task was exhausting. She took his hand gently and placed the badge in it. She spoke softly and distant. "I've had enough of patches for one day. I'm going home."

He examined the badge she gave him. It had a red star embroidered on it.

Lydia began her trek back to her home over at Terrace Hills without saying another word.

Thomas looked from Lydia to Percy and back to Lydia once more. He finally rushed up to Shelly and held out the badge to her. "Here. I don't want it." Once Shelly took it from him he said, "Lydia needs me. I'm going to go home with her, okay?"

81

Shelly nodded. "Take care of yourselves. Keep as many lights on that you can."

"Consider it done, Lady Shelly." Percy sheathed his sword. "I shall be ever vigilant in ensuring everyone's safety."

The boy and his animal waved goodbye, then hurried in order to catch up to his cousin. Once they reached her, Shelly watched as Thomas took Lydia's hand. Content that Lydia had improved, she and Abby wasted little time checking on Quinn.

"Are you okay?" Shelly extended her hand to help them up.

Quinn nodded, exhaled and then took Shelly's offer and hoisted themselves up.

"Yes – thanks for asking. I don't know what happened but it was like being trapped on a merry-go-round and then trying to walk a straight line."

"Do you want to come home with us?" Shelly asked out of concern.

Quinn considered the offer, but voiced concern. "Think they'll make it okay?" They nodded to the departing Lydia and her cousin.

Shelly frowned. "I don't know for sure." She sighed. "I'd follow them but I don't think Lydia can stand to be around me right now. It might be best that I give her some space."

"I'll go make sure they make it safely home. I live out that way anyways. Raincheck?"

Abby and Shelly exchanged nods, then Abby added, "If you feel you'll be okay, I think that's a good idea. We may have defeated one monster, but who knows how many more are out there."

Quinn extended their arms out to Abby. "Do you want a hug before I go?"

"Of course I do!" Abby laughed excitedly and embraced Quinn. After a few moments, they parted.

"How about you, Shelly?" Quinn asked.

Shelly was shaky, jumpy and needed to calm down before she felt she could touch anyone. "Maybe... not right now. Ask me later, okay?"

Quinn nodded with a smile. "Cool." They looked to the darkening sky. "I should go. It was nice hanging out and fighting monsters with you." Quinn waved goodbye and ran off towards the entrance to snag their rollerblades before racing off towards Terrace Hills.

Shelly breathed a couple of heavy sighs. "Let's get out of here, okay?" She beseeched.

Abby pulled a flashlight from her backpack in preparation for the coming night. "I thought you'd never ask. I can't handle any more excitement."

Chapter 12

It had grown dark well before they got back home to Abby's house. No one was there. A note sticking out from between the door and the frame provided them some relief. Abby grabbed it before hustling inside, Shelly following quickly after. As soon as they had cleared the door, Abby shut it and locked it.

Abby shook out the jitters. "I hate the dark."

She passed the beam of her flashlight around the house to make sure there weren't any monsters hiding in the corners. Satisfied, Abby shined her light back in Shelly's direction.

"This is going to sound silly, but can you help me move something in front of the door?"

Shelly nodded, still wary from having to keep watch for anything dangerous outside. "I think that's a great idea."

Abby pointed at a loveseat and commanded it to float. The two of them hastily moved it through the living room and up to the door where they set it in place.

"Stop." Abby called out as the loveseat was now anchored in place by her power. "Phew." She said with relief. "That's not going anywhere." She thought for a moment in worry, then looked towards the kitchen. "There's a backdoor too. We could put the table in front of it?"

Shelly nodded and helped light the way as they both cautiously walked down the hallway and into the kitchen. Thankfully, it was empty though it still smelled like French fries.

"Fry sauce." Abby said with a giggle that helped Shelly to relax.

With a quick motion of her hand, the kitchen table levitated off the ground and bonked into the chairs. Together, the girls each grabbed an end and they braced it against the backdoor. Abby called for it to stop and the table froze in place.

Finally feeling safe, Abby slid down the table and onto the floor. She leaned against the wood, trying her best to breathe. Shelly, being as exhausted as she was, decided to join her. They both placed their flashlights on the floor next to them, ensuring that the light pointed towards the living room so they could see if anything was coming for them.

"So here we are again: in a kitchen, having just slain another monster." Abby swallowed hard. Her hands hadn't stopped shaking since she'd got on her bicycle to go home. She tucked them beneath her legs to keep them still.

"Having saved Lydia, yet again..." Shelly added as she leaned her hoop against the wall next to her.

"Do you think that everyone got home okay?" Abby asked.

"We should probably read the note."

"Oh – right." Abby laughed. "I totally forgot." She pulled up her right hand and realized she had crumpled it. "Whoops." Abby tried to smooth it out and opened it. She eased the note in front of her flashlight so that she could read out loud what it said: "*Looked everywhere. No luck. Everyone is safe. I hope you found her. Stay safe. –*

Ximena Mendoza."

"That answers that." Shelly sighed as she placed a hand over her heart to quell her worrying.

"It was a monster, Shell." Abby blinked a few times. "I mean... not like Alex was. A real monster."

"I know."

"How did this happen? My parents were watching TV. Just in that room." She pointed at the living room. "I went to bed early to read a little. My biggest concern was being bullied at school and if Nancy Drew was going to figure out what happened to Helene and Henri Fontaine."

"Did she find out what happened?" Shelly asked in order to keep their conversation from becoming too eerie.

"Huh?" Abby was caught unaware. "Oh – yeah, it all worked out." She stared into the shadows beyond the beams of light from their flashlights. "What are we going to do? How safe are we? How safe is anyone?!"

"I don't know." Shelly shook her head. "I do know one thing..." Shelly linked her arm with Abby's. "I'll do everything I can do protect us."

Abby laid her head onto Shelly's shoulder and whispered tiredly. "I believe you."

A few moments passed and Abby's stomach growled. She chuckled. "My tummy demands tribute." Her laugh was enough to infect Shelly. They both giggled and the world didn't seem so awful.

"I picked up nuts, rice, jerky, granola bars, dried fruit, peanut butter and bread. Which do you want?" Shelly recalled the items off the top of her head while she craned her

GRETAL TRAIL MIX
BIG WOLF JERK
32 OZ
MAY CONTAIN SOME BONE & HAIR
BIG WOLF JERK
32 OZ
MAY CONTAIN SOME BONE & HAIR.

neck to see all the things she had Thomas empty out onto the counter earlier to confirm.

"How about some jerky and granola? I don't know if I can eat much more than that."

Shelly untangled herself from her best friend and made her way to their food pile. "After we eat we should probably go to sleep."

"If we can sleep." Abby expressed with a frown.

Shelly nodded. "We'll try, okay?" She set aside the items they were going to have for their dinner, then returned to her friend to give her a hand up off the floor.

"That's all we can ever do." Abby offered as she took Shelly's hand and returned to her feet. "I'm starving. Let's eat."

After dinner, Shelly and Abby changed into some pajamas. Shelly hadn't brought an overnight bag, but she had some clothes waiting from a past sleepover.

Abby had rounded up some candles from the living room and they lit all of them. They placed them on Abby's dresser in her bedroom and some on the hall table in case one of them needed to use the bathroom in the middle of the night. The room danced with light, under normal circumstances, it would have been a treasured occasion.

They both climbed into bed and pulled the covers up to their necks. They listened to the silence of the world before Shelly started to drift off.

"Shell?" Abby asked while staring at the ceiling.

"Hmm?" She replied, fighting that pull of slumber.

"Lydia burned that monster with light. Is that why monsters are scared of it? Just like Frysauce said?"

Shelly was barely awake. She took a big breath in. "Monsters are scared of light..." She muttered. "Lydia burned it up."

Abby clutched her blanket tightly. "Shell?"

She didn't get a response, just slow breathing as Shelly slept.

"Goodnight, Sun." Abby whispered as she closed her own eyes.

Shelly was in the living room of her own home. The TV showed that same "Standby" message that it had the day before. Her father played with the remote trying to get a different channel, but each one he flipped showed the same thing.

"I don't know what to tell you, Shelly Bean. It looks like we're stuck with what we got." He said as he tried a few more channels.

"What does it mean?" She asked, partially in a daze.

"Well? I suppose we'll have to fend for ourselves. I'm sure there are other ways to spend the day."

He changed the channel once more and the message read as "ybdnatS". Neither of them seemed too concerned about it.

"Wait..." Shelly examined her surroundings. "Where's mom?"

Her father gave her a wry grin. "Don't you remember, sweetheart?"

Shelly shook her head innocently.

"Where mom usually goes... to her secret lair under the house." He laughed.

"Dad!" She playfully smacked his arm.

"I'm sorry, honey. Your mom's a mad scientist. She's been planning on taking over the world for years and she's very close. Any day now."

"I hope it's with breakfast. I really miss her breakfast." Shelly cheerfully admitted.

His smile drained from his face. "Shelly...? I think there's something outside the window."

Shelly laughed again. "You can stop now. I'm not buying that one."

Her father kept his serious face. "There's something outside the window."

Chapter 13

Abby shook her. "Shell – there's something outside the window, please wake up!"

Shelly blinked a few times and the room, as well as her best friend, came into focus. Abby was very distressed.

"Abby...?" Shelly felt a bit disoriented. Her dream had been so vivid. Finding herself back in Abby's room made her feel as though she'd unknowingly walk through one of Max's portals.

She sat up and rubbed her eyes. Abby didn't wait for her to get adjusted for her to completely wake up. She grabbed Shelly's hand and pulled her over to the window. She pointed at the pane of glass, down and towards the street. Abby's room was on the second floor and they could see most of her neighbor's houses.

There, standing in the middle of the street was a tall lanky figure. The light of the moon illuminated the figure from behind, casting its entire front in shadow. Still, they recognized two pinpricks of red light burning where its eyes should have been. It appeared to be the size of an adult, at least a foot taller than Shelly.

It looked up at them, and immediately they ducked beneath the frame. Shelly's heart was pounding again; it was so hard and loud in her ears that she worried the figure would hear her. Abby's eyes appeared like they were going to pop out of her head. She struggled with her breathing. Shelly worried she might hyperventilate.

"What is it? Why is it here?" Abby struggled in whisper.

"I don't know!" Shelly retorted as quietly as she could.

Shelly took a couple of breaths, steadied her resolve, and peeked back over the window sill to see if it was still there.

The man, or what she believed was shaped like a man, had turned its back. From the darkness of the neighborhood, a couple of squat creatures rushed up to it on all fours, using their knuckles to swing themselves forward.

"Are those monsters Frysauce warned us about?" Shelly asked as Abby poked her head high enough to see.

One of the monkey-like creatures pointed to a house and then communicated something silently to the figure. The other one pointed to Abby's house.

"What are they doing?" Shelly asked as she tried to keep out of sight.

"I think they are pointing where kids are. They have to be." Abby bit her nails.

The one in the suit nodded and then dismissed them with a wave of its hand. The creatures turned and sprinted down another street where handfuls of other shadowy creatures joined them.

"What does it mean?" Abby repeated from before.

"I don't know... but I'm sure it isn't anything good."

"They know where I live." Abby shuddered. "I don't think we should stay here anymore."

Shelly nodded. "We can go back to my house tomorrow and figure things out from there."

They rested on Abby's porch, feeling the sun on their skin as it rose in the east. The battery powered clock in Abby's living room kept the time. It was about 8 a.m. Their eyes were a bit droopy, still tired from the scare they had last night.

Shelly and Abby jumped when Abby's front door opened. Shelly's hand instantly snatched up her hula hoop that was resting nearby. Out walked Max and his sister Ximena from a glowing portal. Ximena wore a pretty black dress with purple lace. It looked like one a doll would wear. She followed closely behind her brother with her parasol. Shelly and Abby both sighed with relief.

"Debes pedrile si está bien, usar de su Puerta principal." Ximena expressed harshly to her brother.

"It's fine! They don't care." He replied back dismissively.

"Estás grosero." She warned.

Max turned away from her and rolled his eyes.

"It's okay. I don't mind." Abby spoke up. "A little warning would have been nice though. Are you able to knock first?"

Shelly had no idea what the siblings had said. She was beginning to wish she hadn't switched from Spanish to German.

"I told you to knock." Ximena scolded. The portal behind her faded away once she closed the door behind them.

"Okay! Geez!" He pulled his collar up on his brown leather jacket he wore to block her out. "I'll knock."

His sister just shook her head and walked up to Abby with a wrapped package.

"What's this?"

"Marzipan candy. It's for being a good hostess yesterday. Javier and I greatly appreciate that you invited us."

Abby blushed a bit as she took the present and opened it to see what the candy looked like. "This is lovely, thank you." She paused. "Do you want some?"

Ximena cut off her brother before he could squeeze out a 'yes'. "No thank you. We have some back at home. Those are for you to enjoy."

Max was annoyed that her sister refused him the opportunity to have candy, but was quickly distracted by the way Abby and Shelly appeared. "You two look tired. You okay?"

Shelly shook her head. "We didn't sleep well. Did you two see the strange man with monkey creatures last night?"

"No – we slept the entire night." Max said with interest. "What did he look like? What was he doing?"

Shelly explained what happened and both the Mendoza's latched onto her every word.

"You think he was counting children? I can only guess at why." Max wondered.

"Probably to take inventory of its food." Ximena added. "That's what I would do if I was a monster."

"And I thought I couldn't get more scared." Abby confessed as she wrapped her arms around her knees.

"Maybe Frysauce knows more. He mentioned them yesterday he had seen them." Shelly pointed out.

Ximena sat down on the porch swing and crossed her legs. "Did you ever find Bigfoot?" She asked with a grin.

"You mean Lydia? We found her at the park where we fought a monster—"

"Hey losers!" Came a voice like a car wreck.

Lydia, wearing designer running clothes, stood at the sidewalk, where Thomas dismounted his bike and Percy leapt out of his basket.

Ximena blinked a few times, leaned back against the porch swing, and replied, "That's too bad."

"Lydia?!" Shelly felt her voice get caught partially in her throat. "Are-are you okay?" She asked with a raised eyebrow.

"I'm more than okay, I'm me." She gestured to herself. "Oh..." She feigned some concern. "That's too bad... you're still you."

"Really?" Shelly asked as heat started to rise in her cheeks. "We all risked our safety for you yesterday, and you're still going to treat us like nothing happened?"

"I didn't ask you to come after me. I told you to leave me alone and your insistence brought a monster that I had to save *you* from." She flicked her curls behind her. "I'm still waiting for my thank you."

Shelly stood up on the stairs. "Thank you? You should be thanking us."

"That's fine. I guess I'll be the bigger person and just accept that as a thank you."

"Hmph." Shelly growled.

Two other bicyclists skidded their tires on the concrete, tossing dirt and pebbles down the street. They both smiled as they slowly got off their bikes and joined their friend at the sidewalk.

Shelly recognized them as Alyssa Sharmington, a long-haired blonde girl who kept her wild locks in a ponytail and wore her Applewood Middle School volleyball shirt, and Laci Shephard, a sandy haired, blue eyed girl who wore designer scarves even during the summer. Both were Lydia's best friends and partners in crime. They were known as the terrible trio at school. Lydia was bad enough, but when all three traveled the halls and playground, they pretended they owned the place.

"Well, if it isn't Marker Face and Shelly Whine." Alyssa joked as Laci gave her friend an encouraging fist bump.

"What do you want?" Abby asked in hopes of hurrying them along their way.

"Shelly and I still need to finish our business." Lydia taunted.

Shelly felt a pressure build at the front of her head in irritation. "Listen... if this is about Alex—"

"Relax – Shelly *Whiner* – I'm talking about our race. Yesterday it was interrupted and today we're going to finish."

"What? Are you going to swallow a plane this time?" Shelly joked snottily.

Lydia rolled her eyes. "No, stupid, I'm not going to turn into a plane. A little overkill, don't you think? This time I'm going to have my good friend Alyssa level the playing field."

Alyssa walked to the street and stomped on it with her foot. In a flash, a rainbow spilled across the concrete and spread down the street, several houses in length.

Lydia giggled at everyone's surprise as the rainbow scintillated with a variety of colors. To demonstrate, Lydia ran onto the rainbow and, like a bullet, zipped to the other end. With a single step, she returned back where she started.

"Lyssa set up an entire track just for me. Think you have the guts or are you going to try and back out of it like last time?"

Shelly looked to her friends, who all seemed to share that same annoyed face that followed Lydia wherever she went. After everything they had done for her, nothing had changed. She was safe, and as much of a bully as she had been the day before.

"You know what? You show me the track and you're on!"

A deep voice cut through them like a tornado of glass. It echoed with a feminine whisper, as if two people were speaking at the same time. "Oh — we do love a good race.

Lydia nearly jumped out of her skin as a figure appeared from a puff of black smoke, behind her. It wore an old suit with coat tails, which was neatly pressed, with a white collared shirt, and a drooping black bowtie. A straight black cane was gripped tightly in its hand. Its face had the consistency of burlap, with a thick crease down the center where the nose and mouth should be, and two glowing red embers for eyes.

"Allow us to introduce ourselves, we are the masters of the SOK Market. It is so good to see our children in such high spirits; times

97

troubled as they are."

Shelly snatched up her hoop. She placed herself between Abby and the creature. Shelly's veins pumped heavily as she readied herself for a fight. "Everyone get behind me! It's a monster!"

Play the Game!

No Parents. No School. No Rules

Make your own character and join the children of Applewood in your own homemade adventures. Pick up the tabletop roleplaying game today!

Visit us at: nrmbooks.com